Welcome to ALADDIN QUIX!

If you are looking for fast, fun-to-read stories with colorful characters, lots of kid-friendly humor, easy-to-follow action, entertaining story lines, and lively illustrations, then **ALADDIN QUIX** is for you!

But wait, there's more!

If you're also looking for stories with tables of contents; word lists; about-the-book questions; 64, 80, or 96 pages; short chapters; short paragraphs; and large fonts, then **ALADDIN QUIX** is *definitely* for you!

ALADDIN QUIX: The next step between ready to reads and longer, more challenging chapter books, for readers five to eight years old.

Read more ALADDIN QUIX books!

By Stephanie Calmenson

Our Principal Is a Frog!

Our Principal Is a Wolf!

Our Principal's in His Underwear!

Our Principal Breaks a Spell!

The Adventures of Allie and Amy
By Stephanie Calmenson and Joanna Cole

Book 1: *The Best Friend Plan*

Book 2: *Rockin' Rockets*

Book 3: *Stars of the Show*

Our Principal's Wacky Wishes!

BY
**Stephanie
Calmenson**

ILLUSTRATED
BY**Aaron
Blecha**

ALADDIN QUIX

New York London Toronto Sydney New Delhi

To Justin, with love
—S. C.

This book is a work of fiction. Any references to historical events, real people, or real places are used fictitiously. Other names, characters, places, and events are products of the author's imagination, and any resemblance to actual events or places or persons, living or dead, is entirely coincidental.

ALADDIN QUIX

Simon & Schuster Children's Publishing Division
1230 Avenue of the Americas, New York, New York 10020
First Aladdin QUIX paperback edition August 2020
Text copyright © 2020 by Stephanie Calmenson
Illustrations copyright © 2020 by Aaron Blecha
Also available in an Aladdin QUIX hardcover edition.
All rights reserved, including the right of reproduction in whole or in part in any form.
ALADDIN and the related marks and colophon are registered
trademarks of Simon & Schuster, Inc.
For information about special discounts for bulk purchases, please contact
Simon & Schuster Special Sales at 1-866-506-1949 or business@simonandschuster.com.
The Simon & Schuster Speakers Bureau can bring authors to your live event. For
more information or to book an event contact the Simon & Schuster Speakers Bureau
at 1-866-248-3049 or visit our website at www.simonspeakers.com.
Designed by Karin Paprocki
The illustrations for this book were rendered digitally.
The text of this book was set in Archer Medium.
Manufactured in the United States of America 0720 OFF
2 4 6 8 10 9 7 5 3 1
Library of Congress Control Number 2020936154
ISBN 978-1-5344-5756-0 (hc)
ISBN 978-1-5344-5755-3 (pbk)
ISBN 978-1-5344-5757-7 (eBook)

Cast of Characters

Mr. Barnaby Bundy: Principal

Hector Gonzalez: Loves making his friends laugh

Penny Pickel: Library designer

elf: Oak tree resident

Roger Patel: Top student and class leader

Nancy Wong: Plans to be a zoologist

Mr. Charles Strong: School librarian

Ms. Ellie Tilly: Kindergarten teacher

Alice Wright: Kindergartener who always tells the truth

Ms. Marilyn Moore: Assistant principal

Contents

1

Psst!

PS 88 was buzzing with activity. People kept popping their heads into **Principal Bundy**'s office with questions about the **fundraiser** to help fix up the library.

The kids were having fun

planning their programs—talent shows, game shows, comedy acts.

Hector was working on his comedy act.

"Hi, Mr. Bundy!" he said. "Would you like to hear my principal joke?"

"Sure thing," said Mr. Bundy. He always liked to **encourage** his students' efforts. That's just one of the reasons why he's the best-loved principal in town.

Hector began, "What happened when the principal tied

all the third graders' shoelaces together?"

"What happened?" asked Mr. Bundy.

"They took a class trip!" said Hector.

"Good one!" chuckled Mr. Bundy.

Knock, knock. **Penny Pickel** was at the door. She was the **designer** hired to oversee the library makeover.

"Welcome, Ms. Pickel!" said Mr. Bundy.

Hector walked out and Ms. Pickel walked in.

She shared some of her ideas, which included fresh paint, new shelves and better lighting.

"My **proposal** is almost ready," said Ms. Pickel. "Have you a moment to come outside?"

"Of course!" said Mr. Bundy.
"I love getting out on a beautiful
day."

Penny Pickel led Mr. Bundy to
the big oak tree at the side of the
school.

"This tree needs to come down," she said. "It's blocking light from a corner of the library."

"I'm sorry to hear that," said Mr. Bundy. "I really like this tree. In fact, I like all our trees."

"I'm glad you have others since this one needs to go," said Ms. Pickel, looking at her watch. "And now I have to go too. I'll send you my final proposal soon."

She hurried off, leaving Mr. Bundy gazing at the tree.

"Psst! Psst-psst!"

The principal turned to see who was trying to get his attention.

"Yoo-hoo! Over here," called

a voice.

Mr. Bundy saw an **elf** jump out

from behind the tree, looking very

upset.

"We need to talk," said the elf.

"Right now!"

2

It's a Deal!

"This tree is my home," said the elf. "You can't let anyone chop it down."

Mr. Bundy was quite surprised to learn an elf was living on school grounds.

Trying to be polite, he said, "Allow me to introduce myself. I'm Mr. Bundy, the principal of PS 88."

"**I know that!** Didn't I just tell you I live here?" snapped the elf. He certainly had a strong **personality**. "So, are you going to save my tree?"

"Well, it might not be up to me," said Mr. Bundy. "Ms. Pickel is in charge of the project. I don't think I can say no to her."

"Of course you can," said the

elf. "You say, **NO! NO! NO! NO! NO!**" He stamped his feet and beat the air with his fists.

Mr. Bundy was glad the kids weren't outside for recess. This elf was setting a very poor example for his students.

"Look," said Mr. Bundy. "I try my best to get along with everyone, but . . ."

"No buts!" said the elf. "I'll make you a deal."

"What kind of deal?" asked Mr. Bundy.

"If you save my tree, I will grant you one wish. No, make it two. **Wait, three wishes!**" said the elf, not wanting to take any chances.

"Well . . . ," said Mr. Bundy.

"Think of the things you can do for your school," continued the elf. "Or maybe you'd like a new bike. Yours is a little rusty. Or a new suit. I see you're a snappy dresser. How about a trip to Hawaii? A hard worker like you could use a vacation."

"This is quite an attractive

offer," said Mr. Bundy. "May I think about it?"

"No. You. May. Not," said the elf. "I'm going to start counting and when I get to three, I'll need your yes or no. I'll go slowly to give you time to think of all the great things you can wish for."

The elf raised his finger in the air and said, "One Mississippi."

If I take the deal, thought Mr. Bundy, *I can wish for a whole new library this afternoon. I can even wish for a whole new school.*

"Two Mississippi," said the elf, holding a second finger in the air.

That wouldn't work. The kids would ask too many questions, thought Mr. Bundy. *But I could wish for . . .*

"Three Mississ . . . ," said the elf, unfolding his third finger.

He was just about to finish saying Mississippi when Mr. Bundy, not wanting to miss his chance, called, **"It's a deal!"**

"Wise choice," said the elf. Then he tugged his ear three times.

While he was tugging his ear, he chanted:

"Alikazam! Alikazoo!
This magical elf
grants three wishes
to you!"

"You're all set, Mr. B. Enjoy those wishes," said the elf, going back to his tree.

Mr. Bundy headed back into school, hoping he'd made the right choice.

3

First Things First

PS 88 was still buzzing with activity, and now Mr. Bundy's head was buzzing with ideas. He needed to come up with three good wishes to help the school.

"First things first. I've got to

email Ms. Pickel," said Mr. Bundy
to himself. He sat down to type.

Dear Ms. Pickel,
    This is to inform you that
we have decided to keep the
tree in our schoolyard.
    We look forward to seeing
your final proposal.
Sincerely,
Mr. Bundy

Next, he decided to take a spin
around the school to see what he
could wish for. He ran into **Roger**

in the hall. Roger was an excellent student.

"Hi, Mr. B!" said Roger. "I'm hosting a game show for the fundraiser! Want to play?"

"I'm a little busy now," said Mr. Bundy. He wanted to make his three wishes fast. That elf didn't seem very trustworthy and Mr. Bundy worried that he might change his mind.

"I'll be quick!" said Roger. "The **category** is Rhyme Time. I'll tell you the answer and you guess the question. Okay, here's the answer: It's a slow way to send a letter."

"I give up," said Mr. Bundy, hoping to hurry Roger along.

"Snail mail!" said Roger.

"Did someone say snail?" said **Nancy**, who was passing by on her way to the lunchroom. "I'm bringing my snail **collection** to the fundraiser for my Slimy Snails presentation."

Nancy was another excellent student. She planned to be a

zoologist some day. To her, snails were exciting creatures.

"My snails are so cute," said Nancy. "I'm going to bring a tankful."

"I'm tankful . . . I mean thankful that you two have such interesting projects," said Mr. Bundy. "I'd like to hear more, but I've really got to run."

Then he hurried down the hall.

4

Poof!

Passing the library, he decided to stop in and see the problem caused by the elf's tree. It completely blocked the light in one of the reading corners. He had never noticed that before, but there was no turning back now. He'd made a deal with the elf, so the tree was going to stay.

Maybe my first wish could be for a big picture window to bring in more light, thought the principal. *They're very expensive, so we couldn't possibly raise enough money for one.*

Mr. Strong, the librarian, waved to Mr. Bundy. He was in the computer area, helping a group of students. The computers were old and broke down way too often. *New* *computers could be a good second wish,* thought Mr. Bundy.

Across the room, **Ms. Tilly**'s kindergarteners were looking for books to borrow. Suddenly a student named **Alice** started giggling and couldn't stop.

Her classmates gathered round to see what was so funny. Alice showed them a picture of a man with sausages attached to his nose. The children thought this was **hysterical**. Their laughter was music to Mr. Bundy's ears.

"I wish I had a sausage nose to make the children laugh," **mumbled** Mr. Bundy.

POOF!

Oh no! Mr. Bundy's nose did not feel like his nose anymore. He reached up and touched a string of sausages! The principal gasped. Everyone turned to look.

Mr. Bundy spun around so fast, no one saw what had happened to him. He raced down the hall with the string of sausages swinging wildly from side to side.

He'd almost made it to his office without being seen when **Ms. Moore**, the assistant principal appeared.

"Mr. Bundy? What is that? **What's going on?**" Ms. Moore **sputtered**, racing to keep up.

When they reached his office, Mr. Bundy quickly closed the door.

"Is that one of those silly fake noses?" asked Ms. Moore. "Will you be doing a funny act at the fundraiser?"

"I'm afraid not," said Mr. Bundy. "These are real sausages and they're stuck to my real nose."

He told Ms. Moore about his meeting with the elf and his visit to the library.

At first, Ms. Moore was **speechless**. Then she couldn't help it. She burst out laughing.

"You think this is funny, Ms. Moore?" said Mr. Bundy. "Well, I wish you had sausages on your nose too!"

POOF!

Oh no! Now Ms. Moore had a sausage nose just like Mr. Bundy's.

There was a knock at the door. Mr. Bundy and Ms. Moore dove to the floor to hide.

5

A Plan

Roger walked in and saw Mr. Bundy's empty chair. Hearing shuffling on the floor, he looked down.

"There you are, Mr. Bundy! And hi, Ms. Moore!" he said. "Did one of you lose something?"

"Um, why, yes. I seem to have lost a contact lens," said Mr. Bundy.

"I'm helping him find it," said Ms. Moore.

"I didn't know you wore contacts," said Roger.

"They're new. I'm trying them out," said Mr. Bundy.

"I'll help you look," said Roger.

"NO!" called Mr. Bundy and Ms. Moore together.

"Thank you for offering, Roger," said Ms. Moore. "But we have to be careful that no one steps on the lens."

"Right," said Roger, backing out carefully. "I'll come back later. I hope you find it soon."

"Please close the door behind you," said Mr. Bundy.

As soon as the door closed, the timer on Mr. Bundy's phone went off. *Bzzzz-bzzzz! Bzzzz-bzzzz!*

"Is that what I think it is?" said Ms. Moore.

"I'm afraid so," said Mr. Bundy.

"It's time for the assembly. We had planned to talk about the fundraiser. Now I'll have to use my last wish to get these sausages off our noses."

"Wait!" said Ms. Moore. "Don't waste your last wish. We need so many things for the school. Maybe if I talk to the elf, he'll be understanding and help us."

"From what I know of this elf, understanding is not a word that comes to mind," said Mr. Bundy.

"It's worth a try," said Ms. Moore. "I'll skip the assembly. When the coast is clear, I'll run out and see if I can **convince** the elf to help us. If anyone comes along, I'll use my scarf to cover my nose."

"Good idea," said Mr. Bundy. "I've got a handkerchief I can use to cover up. I'll say I feel a cold coming on and don't want anyone to catch it."

Mr. Bundy tied the handkerchief across his nose, then turned to leave.

"Stop!" called Ms. Moore. "You've got a sausage hanging out."

Mr. Bundy tucked in the **stray** sausage and went off to lead the assembly.

6

Goodbye, Hawaii

"Greetings, everyone," said Mr. Bundy. "Please excuse my covered face. I feel a terrible cold coming on. **Ah-ah-choo!**"

"Bless you, Mr. Bundy!" called the students and teachers together.

"Mr. Bundy's having a really hard day," Roger whispered to Nancy and Hector. "First he lost his contact lens and now this."

"I didn't know he wears contacts," said Nancy.

"He told me he was trying them out," said Roger.

"Poor Mr. B," said Hector.

"Several of you have shared your plans for the fundraiser and they've been excellent," said Mr. Bundy. "Our designer, Penny Pickel can start work on the library as soon as we've raised enough money."

Suddenly, Mr. Bundy felt a tickle in his nose. This time, it was a real one. He tried to hold back the sneeze. But it came too fast.

Ah-choo!

The handkerchief flew up. The sausages flopped down.

Eyes popped. Jaws dropped.

Alice burst out laughing. "Mr. Bundy's like the man in my book!" she called.

Without knowing it, Alice had

given him just the **explanation** he needed.

"You're right, Alice," said Mr. Bundy. "That story was so funny, I decided to act it out for the fundraiser."

The kids and teachers started laughing and clapping for their principal, who was willing to help his school any way he could.

Once again, their laughter was music to Mr. Bundy's ears.

He spoke for a short time about how the fundraiser day would be organized, then said, "Back to your classrooms, everyone. **You've got work to do!**"

Once they'd all gone, Mr. Bundy hurried back into his office where Ms. Moore was waiting.

"Did you find the elf? Did you talk to him?" asked Mr. Bundy.

"Yes and yes. But his answer was no," said Ms. Moore. "He said a deal's a deal. Three wishes to a customer. Goodbye."

"Of all the elves in all the towns in all the world, we had to get a crabby one," said Mr. Bundy. "Now there'll be no picture window in the library. No new computers. No trip to Hawaii."

"Trip to Hawaii?" said Ms. Moore.

"Just a little daydream I had," sighed Mr. Bundy. "But now it's time to use my last wish. Here goes. I wish these sausages off both our noses!"

POOF!

Ms. Moore and Mr. Bundy were terribly disappointed to have used up the wishes, but they were

happy being back to normal. And normal at PS 88 was pretty terrific anyway.

"I don't ever want to see a sausage again," said Ms. Moore.

7

Best Wishes

When Penny Pickel first heard that the tree she wanted to cut down was staying up, she wasn't happy.

But Mr. Bundy shared an idea he had. The area shadowed by the tree could have gentle lighting, **comfy** beanbag chairs, and a sign that said COZY CORNER. Ms. Pickel had to agree it was a nice touch.

At the fundraiser, Mr. Bundy and Ms. Moore enjoyed seeing the students' plans in action.

Nancy had an terrific Slimy Snails presentation.

Roger was the perfect game show host.

Hector made everyone laugh with his comedy act.

And Alice had a storytelling

corner. She read *The Three Wishes*, and Mr. Bundy joined her, wearing a silly fake sausage nose.

It was all great fun and many tickets were sold.

Ms. Moore had said she never wanted to see another sausage, but Mr. Bundy had a suggestion she couldn't **resist**.

They had a food stand where they took turns calling, **"Sausages! Get your tasty sausages here!"**

"Veggie or meat! Spicy or sweet!"

They had lots of customers, including Roger, Hector and Nancy.

"This line's really long," said Roger.

"I know, I never sausage a thing," joked Hector.

Roger and Nancy groaned, but Mr. Bundy and Ms. Moore gave Hector's joke two thumbs up.

The fundraiser was a big success. When it was over and everyone was gone, Mr. Bundy heard a familiar voice calling from outside, *"Psst! Psst!* **Over here!"**

The elf was standing beside his tree. Mr. Bundy was not a big fan of the elf, but he went outside anyway.

"I'm sorry I couldn't give you another wish," said the elf. "It's just that . . ."

"I know," said Mr. Bundy. "**A deal's a deal.** Three wishes to a customer, and all that."

"It really wasn't my choice. You see, if I break one of the **Official** Rules for Elves, I get in trouble," said the elf. "But I'm allowed to make a few wishes of my own. Close your eyes and cover your ears. I want this to be a surprise."

Mr. Bundy did as he was told.

When he felt a tug on his jacket, he opened his eyes.

There, set in the shade of the elf's tree, was a beautiful oak reading bench that said, FOR THE CHILDREN OF PS 88. Mr. Bundy could hardly believe it.

"Thank you so much," he said. **"It's amazing!"**

Mr. Bundy sat on the bench and the elf joined him.

"Shall I go get us some books?" asked Mr. Bundy. "We could read together awhile."

"No, thanks," said the elf.

"Don't you like to read?" asked Mr. Bundy.

The elf whispered, "I don't know how."

"We'll just have to fix that," said Mr. Bundy. "I'll teach you."

The principal went into the library and came back with some great books to get them started.

That night, Mr. Bundy listened to his favorite Hawaiian music while eating the pineapple pizza he'd picked up on his way home. It wasn't exactly a trip to Hawaii, but it was just what he wished for.

Word List

category (KAT•uh•gore•ee):
A grouping of things or people

collection (koh•LEK•shun): Items
gathered together for study or
other purposes

comfy (COM•fee): Relaxing to be in

convince (kun•VINSE): To get
someone to believe something

designer (dih•ZYNE•er): A person
who creates a plan for a project

encourage (ehn•KUH•ridge):
To give help, support, or hope

explanation (ex•pluh•NAY•shun):
A reason for doing something

fundraiser (FUND•ray•zer):
An event held to bring in money

hysterical (hih•STAIR•ih•kul):
Extremely funny

mumbled (MUM•bulld): Spoken
quietly in a way that's hard to
understand

official (uh•FIH•shul): Coming
from a known and important source

personality (per•sun•AL•ih•tee):
The set of qualities that make up a
person's character

proposal (pro•POH•zul): A plan or suggestion

resist (ree•ZIST): To not give in

speechless (SPEECH•less): Unable to talk

sputtered (SPUH•terd): Spoken quickly and explosively

stray (STRAY): In the wrong place

Questions

1. If you could make a wish for your school, what would it be?
2. If you could make a wish for yourself, what would it be?
3. If you could make a wish for the world, what would it be?
4. Hector's joke on page 48 is wordplay because "sausage" sounds like "saw such." Can you think of another wordplay yolk? I mean, joke!